Lakota

Treasure Chest Books • Tucson, Arizona

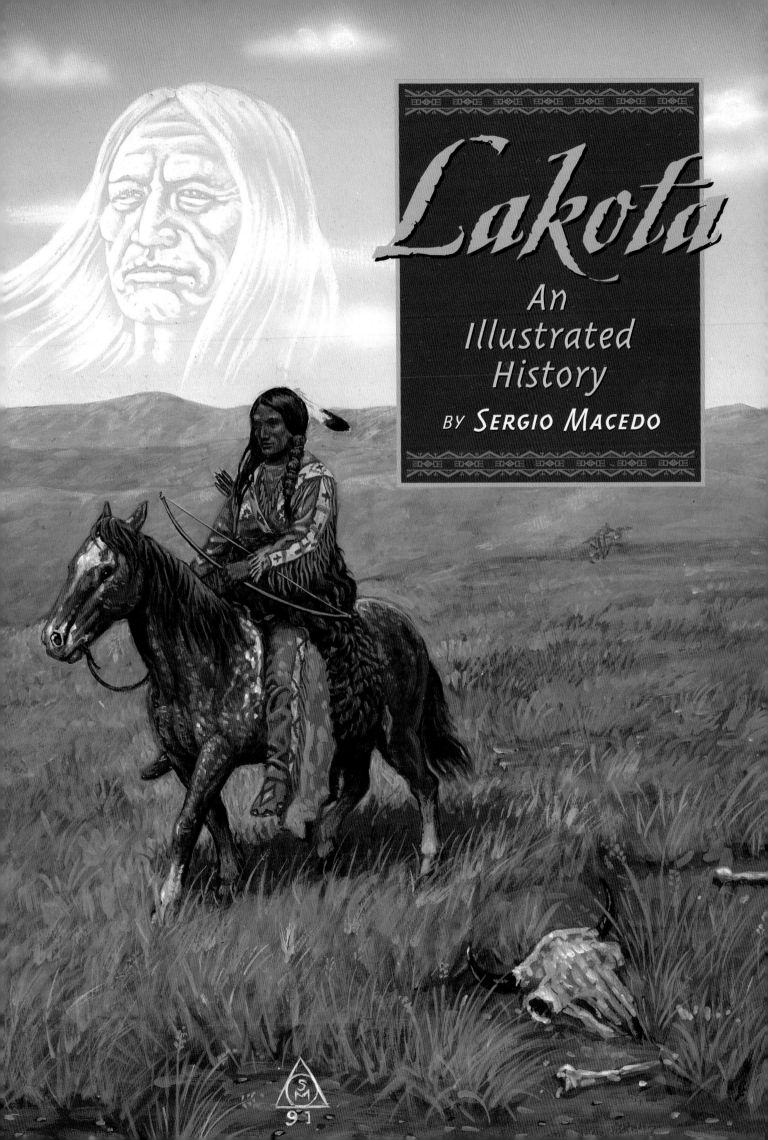

Lakota

An Illustrated History

BY SERGIO MACEDO

This book is dedicated to the
Lakota people in memory of Black Elk.

Thanks to Lee Yatlee for his help with the text.
Also thanks to Gerard Baker, Larry Evers, and Floyd Red
Crow Westerman for their interest and assistance.

TREASURE CHEST BOOKS
P.O. Box 5250, Tucson, Arizona 85703-0250
(520) 623-9558

Copyright © 1996 by Sergio Macedo

Type set in Tekton, Triplex, and Ovidius
Printed in Korea

ISBN 1-887896-02-3   Library of Congress No. 96-61117

Contents

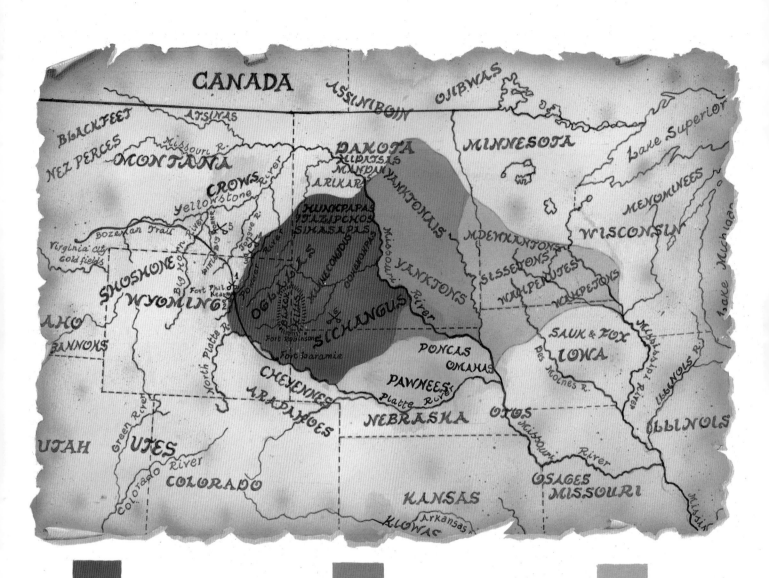

LAKATKO
(LAKOTA)

SICHANGUS
OGLALAS
MINNECONJOUS
ITAZIPCHOS
SIHASAPAS
OOHENONPAS
HUNKPAPAS

NAKATKO
(NAKOTA)

YANKTONS
YANKTONAIS

DAKATKO
(DAKOTA)

MDEWKANTONS
SISSETONS
WAHPEKUTES
WAHPETONS

1. ANNIHILATION OF FETTERMAN, DECEMBER 21, 1866

2. WAGON BOX FIGHT, AUGUST 2, 1867

3. CAVALRY ATTACKS PEACEFUL LAKOTA AND CHEYENNE CAMPS AND IS DEFEATED, MARCH 17, 1876

4. BATTLE OF THE ROSEBUD, JUNE 17, 1876

5. BATTLE OF THE LITTLE BIGHORN, JUNE 25, 1876

6. MASSACRE AT WOUNDED KNEE, DECEMBER 29, 1890

MY SON... REMEMBER THAT THE REAL WORLD IS BEYOND THIS ONE. EVERYTHING WE SEE HERE IS SOMETHING LIKE A SHADOW FROM THE **SACRED WORLD.**

I NEVER FORGET TO PRAY TO THE GREAT SPIRIT, MY FATHER, SO THAT ONE DAY I, TOO, WILL HAVE THE KNOWLEDGE TO BECOME A **WICHASHA WAKAN.**[1]

YOU ARE SKILLFUL WITH THE BOW AND A GOOD HORSEMAN. SOON YOU WILL REACH THE AGE TO BE A **LAKOTA** WARRIOR. BUT BEFORE YOU BECOME A HOLY MAN, YOUR MIND MUST MATURE AND YOU MUST SEEK WISDOM.

[1] A SEER-HEALER

ALL THE ANIMALS, BIRDS, TREES, AND PLANTS ARE OUR BROTHERS. THE EARTH IS OUR MOTHER, AND ALL THAT WE DO TO HER, WE ARE DOING TO OURSELVES. IN THE HUNT, ALWAYS THANK THE SPIRIT OF THE ANIMAL THAT NOURISHES YOU.

8

SSSSSSS

THUD!

HEY-A-HEY! WAKAN TANKA HAS HEARD MY VOICE! MAY MY PEOPLE LIVE WITH PLENTY!

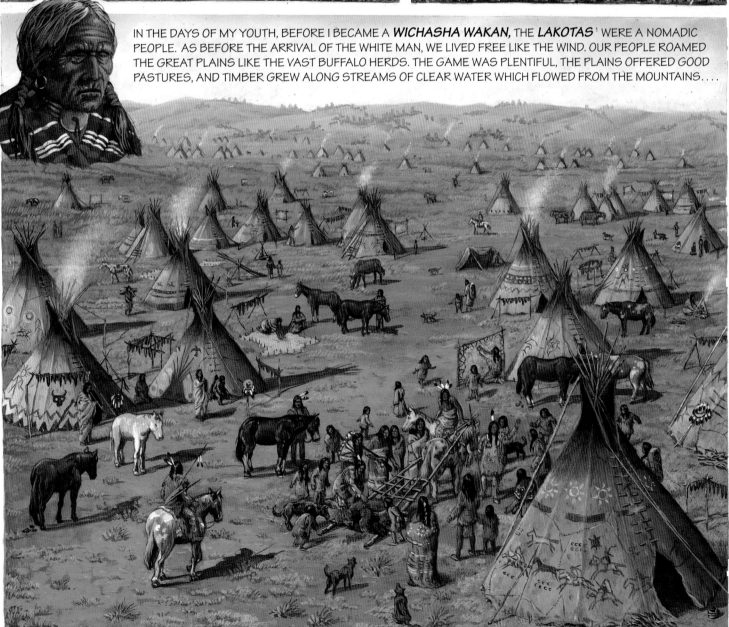

IN THE DAYS OF MY YOUTH, BEFORE I BECAME A **WICHASHA WAKAN,** THE **LAKOTAS**[1] WERE A NOMADIC PEOPLE. AS BEFORE THE ARRIVAL OF THE WHITE MAN, WE LIVED FREE LIKE THE WIND. OUR PEOPLE ROAMED THE GREAT PLAINS LIKE THE VAST BUFFALO HERDS. THE GAME WAS PLENTIFUL, THE PLAINS OFFERED GOOD PASTURES, AND TIMBER GREW ALONG STREAMS OF CLEAR WATER WHICH FLOWED FROM THE MOUNTAINS....

[1] THE **LAKOTAS, DAKOTAS,** AND **NAKOTAS** WERE THE PEOPLE KNOWN BY THE WHITES AS **SIOUX.** THEY WERE DIVIDED INTO SEVERAL SUB-TRIBES AND CLANS. SEE MAP, PAGE 6.

LOOK AT RED HAWK! HE HAS BEEN TRADING WITH THE *WASICHUS.*[1]

I GAVE TWO PONIES FOR THIS GUN... I WILL HUNT MANY BUFFALO WITH IT!

WHITE MEN

BEWARE THE *WASICHUS!* A LONG TIME BEFORE YOU WERE BORN, A *WICHASHA WAKAN* DREAMED THAT A STRANGE RACE HAD WOVEN A SPIDER'S WEB ALL AROUND OUR PEOPLE. THE ANIMALS HAD DISAPPEARED AND WE WERE ALL STARVING IN SQUARE GRAY HOUSES IN A **BARREN LAND**....

THE *WASICHUS* ARE MANY AND HAVE POWERFUL MEDICINE. THEY HAVE INVADED AND TAKEN THE LANDS OF MANY TRIBES TO THE EAST. BEWARE OF THEIR LIES, THEIR DISEASES, AND THEIR *MINNE WAKAN.*[2]

HAVE YOU EVER SEEN THE *WASICHUS,* COUSIN CURLY?[3]

NOT ME, BUT MY FATHER DID. HE DOESN'T LIKE THEM. HE SAYS THEY WANT TO KILL US AND TAKE OUR LAND.

[2] *LIQUOR*   [3] *LATER KNOWN AS CRAZY HORSE*

WHEN I'M OLDER, I'LL LEAD OUR TRIBE IN CHASING THE *WASICHUS* OUT OF OUR COUNTRY!

THEIR MEDICINE SEEMS VERY POWERFUL. THE DAY OF MY *HAMBLECHEYAPI*[4] IS COMING. AFTER PURIFYING MYSELF IN THE *INIPI*[5], I'LL GO TO THE MOUNTAIN TO FAST AND PRAY. MAYBE THE GREAT SPIRIT WILL GIVE ME A POWER STRONGER THAN THEIRS.

I HAD KNOWN FOURTEEN WINTERS AT THE TIME OF MY INITIATION....

TUNKASHILA,[6] **HI-YAY, HI-YAY!** THE POWERS WILL COME TO ME! I HEAR A VOICE! THE **SACRED POWERS** COME TO ME!

[4] *VISION QUEST*   [5] *SWEAT LODGE*   [6] *GRANDFATHER OF GRANDFATHERS*

GRANDFATHER, OH GREAT SPIRIT! I SEND A VOICE TO THE SKY! HEAR ME! MITAKUYE OYASIN![1]

NOW YOU ARE PURIFIED BY THE SACRED STEAM... NOW YOU MAY GO TO THE MOUNTAIN.

WAKAN TANKA! HEAR ME!

[1] I GIVE THANKS TO THE WHOLE CREATION!

SACRED BEINGS, COME TO ME! SACRED SPIRITS, FLY THROUGH THE AIR TO ME! COME TO ME!

SACRED ARE THE TRADITIONS OF THE ANCIENT PEOPLE! I WILL FOLLOW THEM FOREVER! HEAR MY VOICE!

THREE DAYS... AND NO VISION! I'M WEAK... VERY TIRED!

I'M DIZZY, GREAT SPIRIT! I SEND A VOICE IN DESPAIR! HEAR ME, GREAT SPIRIT!...

HEY-A-HEY! YOUNG LAKOTA! BE STRONG! THE SPIRITS CALL YOU!

12

I AM THE **SPIRIT OF THE WEST.** FROM THE THUNDER BEINGS YOU SHALL HAVE MY POWER. THIS IS THE CUP OF LIFE WITH LIVING WATER, THE POWER TO MAKE THINGS LIVE, AND IT IS YOURS. THIS IS THE POWER TO DESTROY, AND IT IS YOURS.

I AM THE **SPIRIT OF THE NORTH,** THE ONE WHO BRINGS SNOW AND CLEANSING WIND. ON EARTH YOU SHALL MAKE A NATION LIVE, FOR THE POWER OF THE PURIFYING WIND FROM THE GIANT'S WING IS YOURS.

I AM THE **SPIRIT OF THE SOUTH,** SOURCE OF THE WINDS OF LIFE. I GIVE YOU THE LIVING CENTER OF YOUR NATION, AND YOU SHALL USE ITS POWER FOR YOUR PEOPLE. THE TREE OF LIFE SHALL STAND IN THE CENTER OF THE NATION'S CIRCLE. BY YOUR POWERS YOU SHALL MAKE IT BLOSSOM.

MY SON, WITH MY POWER, **THE POWER OF THE SKY,** YOU SHALL GO ACROSS THE EARTH, AND THE WINDS AND THE STARS SHALL BE YOUR ALLIES. THIS BEING SHALL ALWAYS FLY OVER YOU AND REMIND YOU OF THE CREATOR'S WISDOM.

I AM THE **SPIRIT OF THE EAST,** WHERE THE LIGHT OF KNOWLEDGE COMES FROM. WITH THIS PIPE, YOU SHALL WALK UPON THE EARTH, AND WHEREVER SICKNESS IS, YOU SHALL BRING HEALTH. WITH THE POWER OF THE SACRED PIPE, YOU SHALL PRAY FOR THE WHOLE CREATION THAT IT MAY LIVE IN HARMONY WITH THE CREATOR.

LOOK AT HIM WHO IS YOUR SPIRIT NOW, FOR YOU ARE HIS BODY. HIS NAME IS **THUNDER EAGLE!**

TAKE COURAGE, SON. MY POWER, THE **POWER OF THE EARTH,** SHALL BE YOURS.... YOU SHALL NEED IT, FOR YOUR PEOPLE WILL FACE GREAT TROUBLES. YOU SHALL WALK ON THE **RED ROAD,** THE ROAD OF HAPPINESS, FROM WHERE THE GIANT *WAZIYA* LIVES[1] TO THE SOURCE OF THE WARM WINDS.[2] BUT IT CROSSES THE **BLACK ROAD,** FROM THE PLACE WHERE THE SUN RISES TO WHERE IT SETS.

[1] NORTH   [2] SOUTH

ON THIS FEARFUL ROAD ALSO YOU SHALL WALK, BUT YOU SHALL HAVE THE **POWER** TO DESTROY YOUR **ENEMIES.** THE POWERS OF THE FOUR QUARTERS OF THE WORLD, OF THE EARTH, AND OF THE SKY, WILL LOOK AFTER YOU.

EVERY LIVING BEING WITH ROOTS OR LEGS OR WINGS WILL HEAR YOU AND BE LIKE YOUR RELATIVES.

GRANDSON... NOW YOU SHALL GO BACK WITH THE POWERS WE GAVE YOU, TO THE PLACE FROM WHERE YOU CAME. **MAKE EVERY DAY A SACRED ONE!**

WAKAN TANKA HAS HEARD MY VOICE!

FROM NOW ON, MY NAME IS *THUNDER EAGLE!*

CRRIYAAHH

I FOLLOWED OUR CUSTOMS. FOR FOUR MOONS AFTER MY VISION, I KEPT IT IN MY HEART. THEN I TOLD MY DREAMS AND VISIONS TO THE *WAAYATAN*[1] AND, ALONG WITH MY WARRIOR TRAINING, I FOLLOWED THE LONG APPRENTICESHIP OF THE *LAKOTA* MEDICINE MEN....

[1] *MEDICINE MAN OF DREAMS AND VISIONS*

CURLY, MY COUSIN AND THE FUTURE CHIEF OF THE *HUNKPATILLA OGLALAS,*[2] MET GUARDIAN SPIRITS IN HIS VISION QUEST ALSO AND TOOK THE NAME OF **CRAZY HORSE**....

[2] *LAKOTA TRIBE*

MY GRANDFATHER WAS A **PEJUTA WICHASHA**[1] AND TAUGHT ME THE POWER OF THE HERBS. BUT MY TRUE MASTER WAS HAWK HEART. HE WAS A HOLY MAN, A GREAT **WICHASHA WAKAN**.[2]

ALL THINGS ARE THE WORK OF **WAKAN TAŃKA.** HE IS IN ALL THINGS... IN THE AIR, THE TREES, THE HERBS, THE RIVERS, THE MOUNTAINS, IN ALL LIVING BEINGS. HE IS ALSO BEYOND ALL THINGS AND ALL BEINGS. WHEN YOU UNDERSTAND THIS DEEPLY IN YOUR HEART, YOU WILL KNOW AND LOVE THE GREAT SPIRIT AND WILL TRY TO LIVE ACCORDING TO HIS WILL.

A LONG TIME AGO, **WAKAN TANKA** SENT A SACRED BEING, THE **WHITE BUFFALO CALF MAIDEN,** TO TEACH US SACRED RITES. SHE BROUGHT TO US THE SACRED PIPE AND TAUGHT US TO PRAY WITH IT, TO BE ONE WITH THE CREATOR.

[1] HERB HEALER   [2] SEER-HEALER

YOUR MIND AND HEART MUST BE HUMBLE AND PURE TO RECOGNIZE THE GREAT SPIRIT IN ALL LIVING THINGS. YOU MUST LEARN TO FEEL THE HEARTBEAT OF MOTHER EARTH, TO TALK TO THE PLANTS... TO HEAR THE VOICE OF ALL ANIMAL CREATURES OF THIS WORLD, FOR EVERY LIVING BEING HAS A   POWER.

EVERYTHING THE POWER OF THE WORLD DOES IS DONE IN A CIRCLE. OUR POWER COMES FROM THE SACRED HOOP OF THE NATION, WHICH IS ITSELF A PART OF THE CIRCLE OF THE WORLD. THE SKY, THE EARTH, THE SUN, THE MOON, AND THE STARS ARE ROUND. THE SUN AND MOON COME FORTH AND GO DOWN IN A CIRCLE. THE HORIZON, THE RAINBOW, THE SEASONS, AND THE LIFE OF A MAN ARE ALSO CIRCLES WITHIN CIRCLES, WITHOUT BEGINNING OR END.

KEEP ON CULTIVATING OBEDIENCE, LISTENING, HONOR, AND RESPECT, GRANDSON. LATER, IT WILL BE COURAGE, GENEROSITY, ENDURANCE, AND WISDOM.... AND WHEN YOU'RE AS OLD AS I AM, THEN YOU WILL CULTIVATE GOODNESS, KNOWLEDGE, LOVE, AND FORESIGHT....

GRANDFATHER, TELL ME ABOUT THE **WASICHUS.**

THE WHITE MAN WAS CREATED BY THE GREAT SPIRIT AND ALSO MAKES PART OF THE LIFE CIRCLE... BUT HE IS OUTSIDE THE SACRED CIRCLE, FOR HE HAS LOST TOUCH WITH THE CREATOR. HE TELLS LIES, HE KILLS FOR PLEASURE... HE IS SICK IN HIS HEART !

SETTLERS, HUNTERS, PROSPECTORS, TRADERS...THE **WASICHUS** CAME FROM THE EAST IN INCREASING NUMBERS ACROSS OUR COUNTRY....

WASICHUS! YOU SAY THAT YOU WANT TO TRADE WITH US AND THEN *GO* ON YOUR WAY....

YOU MAY TRAVEL ACROSS THE COUNTRY OF THE **OGLALA LAKOTAS!** **RED CLOUD** HAS SPOKEN!

BUT IF YOU TALK WITH A FORKED TONGUE AND TRY TO CHEAT US OR TAKE OUR HUNTING GROUNDS, WE WILL KILL YOU AND YOUR SCALPS WILL HANG IN OUR TEPEES!

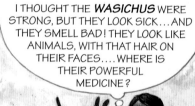

I THOUGHT THE **WASICHUS** WERE STRONG, BUT THEY LOOK SICK...AND THEY SMELL BAD! THEY LOOK LIKE ANIMALS, WITH THAT HAIR ON THEIR FACES....WHERE IS THEIR POWERFUL MEDICINE?

THE BOZEMAN TRAIL[1] CUT THROUGH OUR COUNTRY...AND COUNTLESS **WASICHUS** INVADED OUR HUNTING GROUNDS. THE WARRIORS REACTED....

AS I GREW OLDER, I TOOK PART IN RAIDS AGAINST OUR FOES THE **CROWS** AND **ARIKARAS,** AND ACHIEVED MY FIRST **COUPS**....[2]

[2] WAR PROWESS—TO TOUCH THE ENEMY WITH THE HAND WAS THE GREATEST DEMONSTRATION OF COURAGE.

[1] ROAD ACROSS NEBRASKA LEADING TO GOLD MINES IN MONTANA IN THE 1860S

THE WHITE MAN WAS A THREAT TO THE INDIAN AND TO EVERYTHING THAT LIVED. BUT WE **LAKOTAS** SHOULD HAVE SURVIVED. THE BUFFALO HERDS WERE STILL PLENTIFUL, AND OUR TRIBE STILL FOLLOWED THEIR MIGRATIONS ACROSS THE PLAINS....

HEY-A-HEY!

FORGIVE ME, BROTHER **TATANKA!**[1] I KILL YOU TO MAKE MY PEOPLE LIVE!

YUHOO! YUHOO! YUHOO!

WE'VE GOTTEN MUCH MEAT TODAY. **WAKAN TANKA** HEARD OUR PRAYERS!

[1] BUFFALO

YOU'VE BECOME A GOOD HUNTER, THUNDER EAGLE!

THE SACRED POWERS WERE GOOD TO ME, FAST FOX. DO YOU THINK IT'S ENOUGH TO GET CLAW'S DAUGHTER FOR A WIFE?

MY YOUNG FRIEND, YOU KNOW BETTER THAN I THAT LAUGHING BIRD IS A **WINCINCALA**[2]. HER PARENTS JEALOUSLY GUARD HER...

[2] BEAUTIFUL GIRL

17

LAUGHING BIRD!

THUNDER EAGLE!

WHAT ARE YOU DOING HERE? MY AUNTS MUSTN'T SEE US TOGETHER!

I LOVE YOU, LAUGHING BIRD, AND YOU KNOW IT. I WANT YOU TO BE MY WIFE.

I LIKE TO HEAR YOU PLAYING YOUR FLUTE NEAR MY TEPEE AT NIGHT...BUT YOU KNOW MY PARENTS. THEY ARE VERY STRICT AND DO NOT WANT TO LET ME GO.

WELL THEN, LET'S RUN AWAY!

NO, THUNDER EAGLE...I LOVE YOU, BUT I WON'T DISOBEY MY PARENTS....

I WILL TALK TO YOUR FATHER. I'LL OFFER HIM MY HORSES FOR YOU....

FATHER, I BROUGHT MY HORSES FOR YOU...TWO STRONG STEEDS AND A COLT. THEY ARE VERY GOOD HORSES.

NO.

HOU, THUNDER EAGLE! WHAT'S WRONG, COUSIN? I SEE THE SHADOW OF SADNESS OVER YOU.

HOU, CRAZY HORSE.

MY HEART IS HEAVY, COUSIN. I HAVE ONLY THREE HORSES. I OFFERED THEM TO THE FATHER OF THE ONE I LOVE...AND HE REFUSED!

LET'S GO ON THE WARPATH! THE **PSA**[1] HAVE MANY HORSES...LET'S TAKE THEM, AND YOU'LL HAVE ALL THE WOMEN YOU WISH! *HECHETU WELO!*[2]

[1] THE CROW TRIBE   [2] IT IS SO INDEED!

I JOINED CRAZY HORSE, MANY ARROWS, AND THREE BEARS. NEXT DAY, WE TIED THE TAILS OF OUR HORSES[1] AND LEFT FOR THE COUNTRY OF THE *PSA*....

[1] *WE WENT ON THE WARPATH*

LAUGHING BIRD! I HEARD THAT CRAZY HORSE HAS GONE ON THE WARPATH AGAIN... THAT HE LEFT ON A RAID AGAINST THE *PSA*!

I KNOW IT. THUNDER EAGLE HAS LEFT WITH HIM!

DO YOU THINK THEY'LL COME BACK?

THUNDER EAGLE WILL, I'M SURE...

FOR HE'S COURAGEOUS AND HIS MEDICINE IS STRONG...

THE *WASICHUS* ARE OVERRUNNING OUR COUNTRY! WHERE THEY PASS, THEY DESTROY GAME AND TIMBER, AND THEY LEAVE THEIR DISEASES BEHIND!

THE CHIEFS WHO ALLOW THE **WASICHUS** HERE ARE BAITED AND DON'T SEE THE DANGER. IF WE DON'T ACT, THE **WASICHUS** WILL DESTROY US AND TAKE OUR HUNTING GROUNDS! ALL **LAKOTAS** MUST GATHER TOGETHER TO FIGHT THE INVADERS AND DRIVE THEM OUT!

WE AVOIDED THE **WASICHUS** AND STAYED ON THE TRAIL OF THE **PSA** FOR SIX DAYS....

MANY TRACKS... THEY PASSED HERE YESTERDAY WITH MANY HORSES. THEY MUST NOT BE TOO FAR. LET'S FOLLOW THEM.

WE'LL FIND THEIR CAMP!

TOMORROW, THEIR HORSES WILL BE OURS!

I'LL ATTACK THE CAMP WITH MANY ARROWS AND CREATE CONFUSION AMONG THE TEPEES, WHILE THUNDER EAGLE AND THREE BEARS RUN THE HORSES OFF. LET'S GET READY!

HI YE! MY COUSIN HAS THE COURAGE OF A TRUE LEADER! LET'S PAINT OURSELVES AND CALL FOR THE PROTECTION OF THE GREAT SPIRIT!

NOW, TREMBLE, MY ENEMY! I SEND A VOICE! TREMBLE, IN A SACRED MANNER! ALL YOU WHO SLEEP, TREMBLE!

HOKA-HEY!

AT THE FIRST RAYS OF DAWN....

20

[1] EAGLE

[2] CROW INSULT

22

GREAT SPIRIT! I HAVE KILLED A MAN...AN ENEMY WHO TRIED TO DESTROY US...BUT, WAS IT REALLY NECESSARY TO DESTROY HIS LIFE LIKE THIS?

WE MADE A VICTORIOUS RETURN....

HI-EY-HEY-I-I! REJOICE, LAKOTAS!! WE BRING THE SCALPS AND THE HORSES OF THE ENEMY! HEY-A-HEY!

FATHER, I HAVE SEVEN GOOD HORSES TO OFFER YOU....

IT'S NOT HORSES THAT I WANT, YOUNG BRAVE...

...BUT A COURAGEOUS SON-IN-LAW! YOU HAVE EARNED MY DAUGHTER BY RISKING YOUR LIFE AGAINST THE ENEMY.

LAUGHING BIRD IS FREE TO BE YOUR WOMAN! HECHETU ALOH![1]

[1] IT IS SO INDEED.

THE WINTERS CAME AND WENT AND THE WASICHUS KEPT COMING IN COUNTLESS NUMBERS, KILLING THE BUFFALO AND PROVOKING CONFLICTS WITH THE TRIBES.

WOOUUHH

MY HUSBAND! EVERYONE IS TALKING ABOUT WAR AGAINST THE WASICHUS! THEY SAY THAT ALL LAKOTA BANDS ARE UNITING....

THIS WAS INEVITABLE, MY WIFE! WAKAN TANKA CREATED MAN TO LIVE IN HARMONY, BUT THE WASICHUS ARE DESTROYING OUR WORLD. THE CHIEFS HAVE DECIDED TO FIGHT THE INVADERS!

NOTHING IS SACRED TO THE WASICHUS... THEY DO NOT RESPECT MOTHER EARTH, OR THE SPIRITS OF THE ANIMALS, OR OF ANY LIVING BEING! OUR HOLY MEN KNEW THEY WOULD BRING MISFORTUNE TO OUR PEOPLE....

WE WON'T LET THEM TAKE OUR LAND...WE WILL FIGHT!

WE DID NOT KNOW YET THAT THE *WASICHUS* WERE SO MANY AND SO POWERFUL AND THAT ONE OF THEIR CHIEFS IN WASHINGTON[1] WOULD BE THE ONE TO DECIDE THE **DESTINY** OF OUR **PEOPLE**....

IT'S ABSOLUTELY NECESSARY TO PROTECT IMMIGRANTS ON THE PLAINS, EVEN IF IT MEANS THE EXTERMINATION OF EVERY INDIAN TRIBE TO SECURE SUCH A RESULT!

YOU KNOW, GENERAL, THE ONLY *GOOD* INDIAN IS A DEAD INDIAN!

[1] *GENERAL ULYSSES S. GRANT*

WE MUST ACT WITH VINDICTIVE EARNESTNESS AGAINST THE SIOUX, EVEN TO THEIR EXTERMINATION—MEN, WOMEN, AND CHILDREN. NOTHING ELSE WILL REACH THE ROOT OF THIS PROBLEM!

SO THEN THE SOLDIERS CAME. WITHOUT ASKING OUR PERMISSION, THEY STARTED TO BUILD FORTS ON OUR HUNTING GROUNDS....

THE CHIEF OF ALL THE SOLDIERS WAS A MAN WHO DID NOT LIKE INDIANS, GENERAL WILLIAM TECUMSEH SHERMAN.

WHEN THE *WASICHUS* REALIZED OUR STRENGTH, THEY PRETENDED TO BE FRIENDLY AND CAME TO TALK PEACE....

LAKOTA BROTHERS! I AM YOUR FRIEND AND I SPEAK THE TRUTH! THE CHIEF OF THE SOLDIERS WANTS TO HOLD A COUNCIL WITH THE INDIAN CHIEFS. THE GREAT WHITE FATHER IN WASHINGTON HAS SENT MANY GIFTS TO YOUR PEOPLE.

RED CLOUD, MAN AFRAID OF HIS HORSES,[3] SPOTTED TAIL, AND MANY OTHER CHIEFS WENT TO FORT LARAMIE TO HOLD A COUNCIL WITH THE *WASICHUS*....

[3] *THE WHITE MEN CALLED HIM* **MAN AFRAID OF HIS HORSES**. *HIS LAKOTA NAME WAS* **MAN WHO SOWS FEAR BY HIS HORSES BEING SEEN**.

HOKA-HEY!

OUR WAR CRY ECHOED ACROSS THE PLAINS....

MY GOD! OUTSIDE THE FORT, THE LIFE OF A WHITE MAN IS WORTHLESS!

OUR BANDS GATHERED UNDER RED CLOUD, WITH OUR ALLIES, THE **CHEYENNES** AND **ARAPAHOES**....

THE INDIANS KEEP OUR THREE FORTS ALONG THE ROAD PRACTICALLY UNDER SIEGE, COLONEL CARRINGTON! IT CAN'T GO ON! GIVE ME EIGHTY MEN AND I WILL RIDE THROUGH **THE WHOLE SIOUX NATION!**

CAPTAIN FETTERMAN! REMEMBER THAT OUR DUTY IS TO PROTECT THE SETTLERS, NOT TO START CONFLICTS!

WE WON'T ATTACK THE WAGON TRAIN UNTIL IT IS FAR FROM THE FORT! WHEN THE SOLDIERS COME TO RESCUE THEM, WE'LL LURE THEM TO THE FOOTHILLS...AND AMBUSH THEM THERE....

TWO **CHEYENNES**, TWO **ARAPAHOES**, AND SIX **LAKOTA** WARRIORS WERE CHOSEN FROM AMONG THE BRAVEST MEN. LED BY CRAZY HORSE, THEY LURED THE SOLDIERS INTO THE TRAP. IT WAS A COLD WINTER DAY....

BAM! BAM! BAM!

HEY-A-HEY!

FORWARD, SOLDIERS!! REMEMBER ALL THE FAMILIES KILLED BY THESE SAVAGES! **CHARGE!!!**

¹ ON DECEMBER 21, 1866, CAPTAIN FETTERMAN AND EIGHTY MEN WERE KILLED IN THE BATTLE.

THE MOONS PASSED AND THE WAR CONTINUED. I FOUGHT IN MANY BATTLES, ACCOMPLISHED GREAT FEATS, AND THE NAME OF THUNDER EAGLE BECAME KNOWN AND RESPECTED AMONG OUR PEOPLE.

HOKA-HEY!

BUT WE WERE DEFEATED AT THE **WAGON BOX FIGHT**....[1]

[1] ON AUGUST 2, 1867, THE **LAKOTA** ATTACKED A MILITARY WAGON TRAIN.

CRAZY HORSE LED OUR CHARGE, BUT THE SOLDIERS HAD NEW GUNS [2] AND SHOT FASTER, MUCH FASTER, THAN BEFORE....

HERE THEY COME... **FIRE!!!**

BAM! BAM! BAM!

[2] MODIFIED BREECH-LOADING SPRINGFIELD RIFLES

THEIR GUNS DECIMATED OUR WARRIORS LIKE FIRE BURNING DRY GRASS. I TRIED TO BREAK THROUGH THE CIRCLE OF WAGONS, BUT MY HORSE WAS KILLED AND I WAS WOUNDED....

BAM! BAM!

I LOST CONSCIOUSNESS AND, AS IN A DREAM...

...MY **NAGI** [3] LEFT MY BODY....

[3] SPIRIT

FOLLOW ME.

THUNDER EAGLE... WHEN YOU MET US FOR THE FIRST TIME, WE GAVE YOU THE POWER OF THE **SACRED BOW,** AND NOW YOU USE IT TO DESTROY THE ENEMIES OF THE NATION....

BUT WE ALSO GAVE YOU THE POWERS OF **LIFE, HEALING,** AND THE **SACRED PIPE,** TO BE USED FOR THE GOOD OF YOUR PEOPLE.

THE NATION IS PUSHED TOWARD THE **BLACK ROAD** AND WILL FACE GREAT HARDSHIPS, BUT YOU MUST LEAD IT TO THE **RED ROAD** OF GOODNESS. YOU MUST BE A CHANNEL FOR THE POWERS OF LIFE AND REGENERATION.

WAR HAS KEPT YOU AWAY FROM THE SACRED ROAD OF **WAKAN TANKA**... YOU MUST RESUME YOUR APPRENTICESHIP WITH OLD HAWK HEART.

OFFER YOURSELF TO THE SUPREME FATHER IN THE SUN DANCE. BE AN EXAMPLE TO YOUR PEOPLE... WE WILL LOOK AFTER YOU. NOW GO BACK TO YOUR OWN WORLD.

BE READY TO FOLLOW WITH ALL YOUR SOUL THE PATH WHICH LEADS TO THE CREATOR.

OH!... MY HUSBAND! LAUGHING BIRD'S HEART IS HAPPY AGAIN! YOU'RE GOING TO HEAL!

WE ARE GLAD THAT YOU CAME BACK TO US, MY SON. SINCE YESTERDAY, YOU HAVEN'T MOVED... BUT WE KNEW THAT LIFE WOULDN'T LEAVE YOU.

HAWK HEART HELPED ME TO CARE FOR YOU. WE SMOKED THE PIPE AND SAW THAT YOU'D GONE TO THE SPIRIT WORLD. MAYBE **WAKAN TANKA** WAS SPEAKING TO YOUR HEART.... BUT THE MEDICINE OF THE **WASICHUS** WAS VERY BAD FOR US. WE LOST THE BATTLE... MANY WARRIORS DIED AND MANY ARE WOUNDED.

WE FIGHT FOR THE LIFE OF OUR PEOPLE! BUT I WONDER IF WAR CAN EVER BRING US HAPPINESS.... FIGHTING THE **WASICHUS** HAS FILLED TOO MUCH OF MY MIND. I MUST STAY CLOSE TO HAWK HEART AND LEARN MORE OF **WAKAN TANKA'S** WAYS.

HAWK HEART WAS VERY OLD, BUT HE HAD MUCH GOODNESS AND GREAT WISDOM....

HEAVY CLOUDS HANG OVER THE CIRCLE OF OUR NATION, SON. OUR PEOPLE WANT TO LIVE IN PEACE, BUT THEY ALSO WANT THE BLANKETS, THE BEADS, THE IRON TOOLS...

...AND GUNS FROM THE *WASICHU* TRADERS. AND ALSO THEIR SWEET FOOD, WHICH WEAKENS THE BODY AND THE MIND, AND THE CRAZY *MINNE WAKAN*.[1] THEY RISK FORGETTING THE SACRED CIRCLE AND THE ROAD OF LIGHT THAT LEADS TO *WAKAN TANKA*...

[1] *LIQUOR*

ALL THE LAND FROM THE MISSOURI RIVER TO THE **BIG HORN** MOUNTAINS, INCLUDING THE **BLACK HILLS** AND THE **POWDER RIVER** COUNTRY WILL BELONG TO YOU AS LONG AS **GRASS SHALL GROW AND WATER FLOW.**

AFTER LONG NEGOTIATIONS, MAN AFRAID OF HIS HORSES, LITTLE WOUND, SPOTTED TAIL, AND SEVERAL OTHER CHIEFS TOUCHED THE PEN.[2] BUT AFTERWARD, THE *WASICHUS* BROKE THE TREATY....

WHY SIGN FOR SOMETHING WE'VE ALWAYS OWNED? NO TREATIES WITH THE *WASICHUS*, AS LONG AS THEIR ROAD AND THEIR FORTS REMAIN ON OUR LAND!

RED CLOUD, BIG ROAD, RED DOG, FOUR HORNS, BLACK MOON, SITTING BULL, AND MANY OTHER CHIEFS STAYED ON THE WARPATH...

[2] *TREATY SIGNED AT FORT LARAMIE ON APRIL 25, 1868*

...WHILE WE KEPT HUNTING THE BUFFALO ON OUR REMAINING LANDS....

SOON, ALL OF OUR TEPEES WILL GATHER TOGETHER FOR THE SUMMER. DURING THE *WIWANYANG WACHIPI*[3], I WILL DANCE GAZING-AT-THE-SUN.

WAKAN TANKA WILL HEAR YOUR VOICE.

THE SUN, THE LIGHT OF THE WORLD, I SEE IT COMING. IT BRINGS HAPPINESS TO LIVING THINGS ALL OVER THE EARTH AND THEY REJOICE. *WAKAN TANKA*, I SEND YOU MY VOICE! MAKE MY PEOPLE LIVE!

[3] *SUN DANCE CEREMONY HELD DURING THE SUMMER ASSEMBLY OF LAKOTA CLANS*

WAKAN TANKA, DAWN BRINGS YOUR LIGHT ACROSS THE SKY. YOU SEE OUR PEOPLE HERE. YOU SEE THE FOUR POWERS OF THE WORLD, AND YOU LOOK UPON US IN ALL THE FOUR DIRECTIONS. WE OFFER YOU OUR BODIES. I OFFER YOU MY SUFFERING ON BEHALF OF OUR PEOPLE. GREAT SPIRIT, HAVE PITY ON US, MAKE US LIVE! *HAY HO!*

WAKAN TANKA! BE MERCIFUL TO US! WE WANT TO LIVE! THAT'S WHY WE DO THIS. **THE POWER OF THE BUFFALO IS UPON US! IT'S HERE NOW!!**

THE BUFFALO COMES. HE'S HERE NOW. THE SACRED POWER OF THE BUFFALO IS COMING. IT'S UPON US NOW. THE SACRED POWER IS HERE NOW.

AFTER FOUR DAYS OF FASTING AND PURIFICATION, WE OFFERED TO THE GREAT SPIRIT THE ONLY THING THAT TRULY BELONGS TO US, OUR BODIES. ONCE MORE, OUR SACRIFICE GAVE ENDURANCE AND STRENGTH TO THE NATION, FORTIFYING ITS SACRED CIRCLE....

TETHERED BY RAWHIDE THONGS TO THE SACRED TREE, WE DANCED WITH OUR EYES FIXED ON THE SUN, BLOWING OUR EAGLE-BONE WHISTLES....

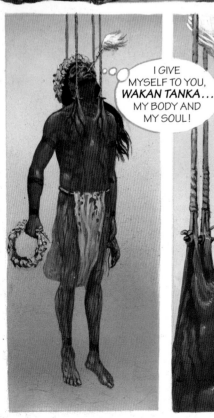

I GIVE MYSELF TO YOU, *WAKAN TANKA*... MY BODY AND MY SOUL!

THUNDER EAGLE! WE ARE WAITING FOR YOU! **COME!**

34

35

GRRROOW!

BROTHER BEAR! HEAR ME! WAKAN TANKA HAS WILLED THAT THIS DAY BE SACRED! I RESPECT YOU... AND YOU MUST RESPECT LIFE! CONTINUE ON YOUR WAY! GO!

GRR

HAWK HEART! HERE!?!

YOU MUST HAVE A PURE HEART, THUNDER EAGLE... FOR THE ANIMALS LISTEN TO YOU! WAKAN TANKA SENT YOU THE BEAR AND NOW, BY ITS POWER AND THE POWER OF THE SACRED PLANT, YOU WILL HEAL.

THE POWERS TOLD ME TO COME HERE, FOR AT THIS PLACE I WOULD FIND THE ONE WHO WILL TAKE MY PLACE AS MEDICINE MAN. I'M GLAD THAT YOU ARE READY, THUNDER EAGLE, FOR MY LIFE IN THIS WORLD IS COMING TO AN END.

NOW, LET'S SMOKE THE PIPE. HE-HETCHETU.

HI-EY-HEY-II! POWER OF THE RISING SUN! POWER OF LIFE-BEARING WINDS! PURIFYING POWER OF COLD WINDS! WINGED POWER OF THE PLACE WHERE THE SUN SETS! POWER OF THE SKY WHERE THE SACRED EAGLE FLIES! POWER OF MOTHER EARTH!

WAKAN TANKA! WE SHALL DO YOUR WILL! WITH ALL BEINGS OF THE WORLD, WE OFFER YOU THIS PIPE. HAY YE! MITAKUYE OYASIN![1]

THIS SMOKE COMES FROM THE EARTH AND REACHES THE SKY. MAY OUR PEOPLE DO LIKEWISE.

NOW YOU ARE THE KEEPER OF THIS PIPE. MAKE A MEDICINE BAG WITH THE SACRED PLANT. WITH THE PIPE, YOU MUST PRAY TO THE GREAT SPIRIT AND HEAL OUR PEOPLE. YOU MUST TEACH THEM ALL THAT YOU HAVE LEARNED FROM ME, FROM YOUR FATHER, OTHER ELDERS, AND YOUR EXPERIENCE.

[1] I GIVE THANKS TO THE WHOLE CREATION.

WHERE MY STEPS STOP, YOURS WILL BEGIN. WHERE YOURS STOP, YOUR SUCCESSOR'S WILL BEGIN. WHEN YOU HAVE TAUGHT THE ONE WHO WILL REPLACE YOU, GIVE HIM THIS PIPE. UNTIL THAT DAY, BE A WORTHY KEEPER OF THIS SACRED OBJECT!

NOW, MY HEART IS LIGHT. I CAN SOON GO TO THE OTHER WORLD....

WAKAN TANKA WAS WITH US. BY AUTUMN, THE SOLDIERS LEFT OUR COUNTRY AND WE BURNED THEIR FORTS....

HEEIII!

IIIHH!

IT WAS A GREAT VICTORY. RED CLOUD SIGNED A TREATY[2] IN WHICH THE WASICHUS PROMISED TO RESPECT THE LANDS OF THE...

...LAKOTAS, THE CHEYENNES, AND THE ARAPAHOES.

WHITE MAN! WE WILL NO LONGER MAKE WAR! FROM NOW ON, WE WILL WALK A ROAD OF PEACE WITH MY PEOPLE!

ALL THAT WE WANTED WAS TO CONTINUE TO LIVE FREE AND HAPPY ON OUR LAND....

[2] TREATY SIGNED ON NOVEMBER 5, 1868, AT FORT LARAMIE.

HAWK HEART DIED THAT WINTER. HE HAD ALWAYS LIVED IN A SACRED MANNER, AND OUR PEOPLE LOVED HIM.

HE HAD GIVEN ME HIS KNOWLEDGE, AND I FOLLOWED HIM AS MEDICINE MAN. WITH THE POWERS OF THE BEAR AND THE SACRED PLANT AND THE SIX GRANDFATHERS OF THE WORLD, I BEGAN TO HEAL OUR PEOPLE.

HEY-A-HEY! GREAT SPIRIT! SUPREME FATHER! TO YOU AND TO ALL POWERS, I SEND A VOICE FOR HELP!

WE ARE WITH YOU, THUNDER EAGLE! ALWAYS KEEP YOURSELF PURE SO THAT THE POWERS OF **LIFE** AND **REGENERATION** MAY REACH THOSE IN NEED.

IN REALITY, IT WAS NOT I WHO HEALED, BUT THE POWERS OF THE SACRED WORLD WHO HEALED THROUGH ME... AND THEY HELPED MANY PEOPLE.

THUNDER EAGLE IS A GREAT HEALER!... EVERYBODY IN OUR CAMP SAYS THAT!

DON'T LET YOURSELF BE MISTAKEN, MY WIFE. EVERYTHING I DO IS BUT THE WORK OF THE **GREAT SPIRIT**.

WHEN EVERY MAN UNDERSTANDS THAT HE, TOO, CAN BE GUIDED BY THE SACRED POWERS OF THE WORLD, THEN MAYBE WE WILL LIVE IN A WORLD OF GOODNESS AND HAPPINESS....

LAUGHING BIRD...

...IS PROUD OF THUNDER EAGLE. I'M READY TO GIVE YOU ANOTHER CHILD.

UNDER PRESSURE FROM THE *WASICHUS*, THE SACRED CIRCLE OF OUR PEOPLE STARTED TO BREAK AND SCATTER. RED CLOUD'S BAND SETTLED ON THE RESERVATION, AND MANY *LAKOTAS* TRADED THEIR FREEDOM FOR THE RATIONS ISSUED AT THE AGENCIES....

BUT MOST OF US STAYED ON OUR TRADITIONAL HUNTING GROUNDS, FOLLOWING THE BISON....

ALL THE INDIANS OUTSIDE THE RESERVATIONS ARE HOSTILE AND SHOULD BE EXTERMINATED!

THE BUFFALO IS THEIR MAIN SOURCE OF FOOD AND MATERIALS. IF WE DESTROY THE HERDS, STARVATION WILL FORCE ALL THE REDSKINS INTO SUBMISSION.

THE RAILROAD WILL MAKE OUR TASK EASIER.... GENTLEMEN, WE'LL INVITE SPORTSMEN TO COME **HUNT BUFFALO**!

THE **IRON HORSE** INVADED OUR COUNTRY. IT BROUGHT AS MANY *WASICHUS* AS THERE ARE LEAVES ON THE TREES...AND DEATH!

AAYEEEAAHH!
IS THE WHITE MAN CRAZY? WHY DOES HE PERSIST IN DESTROYING LIFE? *TATANKA*[1] IS OUR BROTHER! HE'S OUR FOOD, OUR SHELTER! HE IS SACRED!

[1] BUFFALO

IN THE OLD DAYS, BUFFALO COVERED THE PLAINS LIKE GRASS. NOW THEY ARE DISAPPEARING, SLAUGHTERED BY THE **WASICHUS.** THE ANCIENT PROPHECY IS COMING TRUE...

...THE CIRCLE OF OUR PEOPLE IS BROKEN. WE FORGET THE TRADITIONS OF OUR FATHERS. QUARRELS DIVIDE US, AND MANY GO BEG FOR FOOD AND CLOTHES AT THE AGENCIES.

THE **WASICHUS** HAVE BEWITCHED RED CLOUD, MAKING HIM SEE THROUGH THEIR EYES.... BUT WE MUST NOT FORGET WHAT HAS HAPPENED TO OTHER TRIBES...

...WHO HAVE SIGNED TREATIES WITH THE WHITE MAN.

WHERE ARE THEIR LANDS TODAY?

THE ANIMALS, THE PLAINS, THE FORESTS, THE RIVERS, THE MOUNTAINS WERE ALL CREATED BY **WAKAN TANKA**... THEY ARE SACRED! WE MUST PREVENT THE **WASICHUS** FROM DESTROYING THEM! THE **LAKOTAS** MUST STAY UNITED, OR THE SOLDIERS WILL KILL US. THE **WASICHUS** WANT WAR... THEY'LL HAVE IT! SITTING BULL HAS SPOKEN!

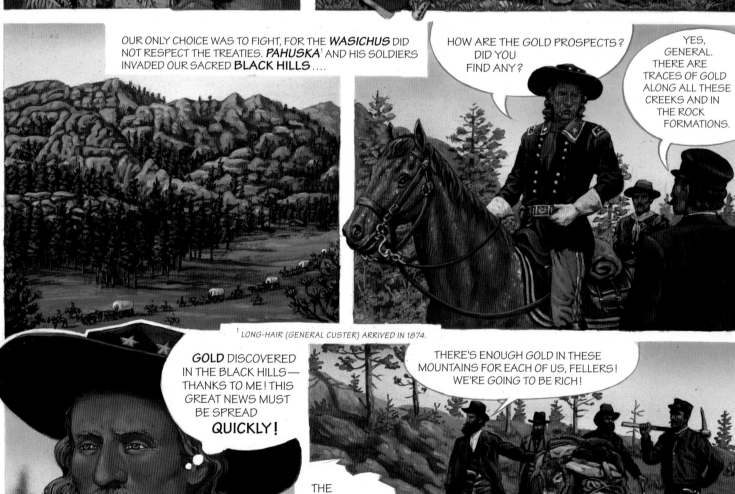

OUR ONLY CHOICE WAS TO FIGHT, FOR THE **WASICHUS** DID NOT RESPECT THE TREATIES. **PAHUSKA**[1] AND HIS SOLDIERS INVADED OUR SACRED **BLACK HILLS**....

HOW ARE THE GOLD PROSPECTS? DID YOU FIND ANY?

YES, GENERAL. THERE ARE TRACES OF GOLD ALONG ALL THESE CREEKS AND IN THE ROCK FORMATIONS.

[1] LONG-HAIR (GENERAL CUSTER) ARRIVED IN 1874.

GOLD DISCOVERED IN THE BLACK HILLS — THANKS TO ME! THIS GREAT NEWS MUST BE SPREAD **QUICKLY!**

THERE'S ENOUGH GOLD IN THESE MOUNTAINS FOR EACH OF US, FELLERS! WE'RE GOING TO BE RICH!

THE PROSPECTORS RUSHED TO OUR SACRED MOUNTAINS LIKE HUNGRY WOLF PACKS....

40

THE *WASICHUS* WERE THE FIRST TO STRIKE IN A SURPRISE ATTACK ON THE CAMP OF TWO MOONS AND HIS *CHEYENNES* AND ON THE CAMP OF HE-DOG AND HIS *LAKOTAS*, WHO WERE PEACEFULLY GOING TO THE RESERVATIONS. THE WARRIORS DROVE OFF THE SOLDIERS, BUT THEIR LOSSES WERE HEAVY....[1]

I HAVE TRIED TO BE YOUR FRIEND, WHITE MAN! BUT STILL YOU ATTACK US AND KILL OUR WOMEN AND CHILDREN.... PEACE WITH YOU IS IMPOSSIBLE!

[1] ON MARCH 17, 1876, COLONEL J. J. REYNOLDS WITH THREE COMPANIES OF CAVALRY ATTACKED A FRIENDLY CHEYENNE AND LAKOTA CAMP.

THAT SUMMER, ALL OUR BANDS GATHERED TOGETHER, ALONG WITH OUR ALLIES, THE *ARAPAHOES* AND *CHEYENNES*. EAGER TO FIGHT, MANY YOUNG MEN CAME FROM THE AGENCIES TO JOIN US....

IN THE SUN DANCE, SITTING BULL, THE GREAT HOLY MAN OF THE *HUNKAPA LAKOTAS*, OFFERED A HUNDRED PIECES OF HIS FLESH TO *WAKAN TANKAN*....

HE DANCED UNTIL HE WAS FALLING FROM EXHAUSTION, AND THEN HE HAD A VISION...

I SAW MANY SOLDIERS FALLING INTO THE CAMP!

EYAH!

HOKA-HEY!

BAM!

YAAAHHH!

LAKOTAS! BACK TO CAMP, TO PROTECT OUR WOMEN AND CHILDREN IF THE SOLDIERS COME!

CRAZY HORSE IS A GREAT WAR CHIEF!

BAM!

WE WERE CAMPED NEAR THE ROSEBUD RIVER WHEN THE SOLDIERS OF *THREE STARS*,[2] WITH *CROW* AND *SHOSHONE* SCOUTS, ATTACKED. AFTER A HARD FIGHT, WE DROVE THEM OFF....[3]

[2] THE LAKOTA NAME FOR GENERAL GEORGE CROOK   [3] JUNE 19, 1876

WE MOVED OUR CAMP TO THE *GREASY GRASS*.[1] ALL THE *LAKOTA* TRIBES WERE THERE... *OGLALAS, HUNKAPAS, MINNECONJOUS, SHICANGUS, ITAZIPCHOS, SIHASAPAS,* AND *OOHENOMPAS,* ALONG WITH THE *SANTEES*,[2] THE *YANKTON*,[3] AND OUR *CHEYENNE* AND *ARAPAHOE* ALLIES. IT WAS OUR BIGGEST GATHERING OF TEPEES...

[1] LITTLE BIG HORN   [2] DAKOTA TRIBE   [3] NAKOTA TRIBE

THUNDER EAGLE SEEMS ABSORBED IN HIS THOUGHTS... SPEAKING TO THE SPIRIT WORLD?

I LISTEN TO THE WIND, THE GRASS, AND THE BIRDS.... ALL TELL ME THAT SOMETHING TERRIBLE IS GOING TO HAPPEN. EAGLE SHOWS ME SOMETHING....

I SEE A CLOUD OF DUST... HORSEMEN ARE APPROACHING OUR CAMP.... *WASICHUS!*

THE SOLDIERS ARE COMING!

CHARGE! GODDAMN 'EM!

F. REMINGTON

TWO CAVALRY BANDS ATTACKED OUR CAMP. THE LARGEST ONE WAS LED BY *PAHUSKA*....[4]

[4] ON JUNE 25, 1876, CUSTER LED THE 7TH CAVALRY IN ATTACKING THE *LITTLE BIG HORN* CAMP.

HOKA-HEY! TAKE COURAGE, LAKOTAS! THIS IS A *GOOD* DAY TO DIE!

OUR QUICK REACTION DROVE OFF THE FIRST CHARGE.[5] THE SOLDIERS WITHDREW, LEAVING THEIR DEAD AND WOUNDED. THEN, LED BY GALL, TWO MOONS, CRAZY HORSE, LOW DOG, AND OTHER CHIEFS, WE ATTACKED *PAHUSKA'S* MEN....

[5] MAJOR RENO'S DETACHMENT

WE RACED TOWARD THE SOLDIERS AND BROKE THEIR RANKS, SHOWERING THEM WITH ARROWS AND BULLETS. *PAHUSKA* WAS AMONG THE FIRST TO FALL. HE LAY FORGOTTEN WHILE THE SOLDIERS FOUGHT DESPERATELY ON THE HILLTOP. WE WERE DRIVEN BY RAGE AND DESPAIR… FOR WE KNEW THEY HAD COME TO DESTROY US….

HEY-A-HEEY!

THEY'RE ALL DEAD!

THE BATTLE ENDED IN A HAND-TO-HAND FIGHT. WE KILLED EVERY ONE OF THEM DOWN TO THE LAST MAN.[1] THE VISION OF SITTING BULL HAD COME TRUE….

[1] CUSTER AND 266 SOLDIERS WERE KILLED IN THE BATTLE OF LITTLE BIG HORN.

MUCH BLOOD HAS BEEN SHED. WHEN WILL THIS CRAZINESS CEASE? **GRANDFATHERS OF THE WORLD!** WHEN WILL WE BE ALLOWED TO LIVE IN PEACE IN OUR OWN LAND?

TAKE COURAGE, SON, AND GUIDE YOUR PEOPLE TO THE GREAT SPIRIT, FOR A TIME OF DARKNESS IS AHEAD. THE NATION WILL FACE THE TERRIBLE HARDSHIP OF THE **BLACK ROAD.**

THE GLORIOUS DAYS OF VICTORY WERE FOLLOWED BY SAD DAYS OF DEFEAT. MANY TROOPS CAME TO FIGHT US, ALL WELL SUPPLIED WITH AMMUNITION AND FOOD. THEIR NUMBERS NEVER SEEMED TO LESSEN… WHILE EVERY WARRIOR WE LOST, WE LOST FOREVER. OUR PEOPLE STARTED TO SCATTER. HUNGRY AND WEARY, MANY LAKOTAS UNTIED THEIR HORSES' TAILS[1] AND WENT TO THE AGENCIES….

[1] LEFT THE WARPATH

WHAT? THE **PAHA SAPA** AND ALL THE COUNTRY WEST OF THEM HAVE BEEN **SOLD** TO THE **WASICHUS**?

THE WASICHUS HAVE PERSUADED THE AGENCY CHIEFS TO PUT THEIR MARKS ON THE TREATY. MAYBE THEY'RE CRAZY FROM **MINNE WAKAN**.[2]

ONLY CRAZY OR VERY FOOLISH MEN WOULD SELL THEIR MOTHER EARTH!

AND SO WE LOST OUR SACRED MOUNTAINS….

[2] LIQUOR

A HARD WINTER CAME EARLY. WHEREVER WE WENT, THE SOLDIERS, WELL SUPPLIED BY THEIR WAGON TRAINS, CAME TO KILL US….

OUR HAPPY DAYS WERE GONE. PURSUED BY THE SOLDIERS, WE WENT DEEPER INTO OUR COUNTRY. IT WAS A TIME OF HUNGER. THE BUFFALO WERE GONE AND OTHER GAME WAS HARD TO FIND. WE ATE OUR HUNGRY PONIES….

THE POWERS FORESAW THIS…. WE ARE ON THE **BLACK ROAD**!

AFTER A HARD FIGHT, SITTING BULL, GALL, AND THEIR BAND LEFT FOR **GRANDMOTHER'S LAND**.[3] MANY OTHERS LEFT US, BUT CRAZY HORSE KEPT RESISTING….

COUSIN, YOU KNOW LIKE ME THAT, WITH THE DEATH OF OUR BROTHERS—THE BUFFALO—THE **LAKOTAS** TOO WILL BE A DYING PEOPLE. BUT I PRAY TO THE POWERS AND MAKE PLANS FOR THE GOOD OF OUR PEOPLE.

[3] QUEEN VICTORIA'S COUNTRY, CANADA

THE WINTER IS TOO HARD AND THE SOLDIERS ARE CLOSE UPON US. THE WOMEN AND CHILDREN STARVE AND FREEZE. I SEE THEIR EYES ASKING HOW LONG WE MUST GO ON THIS WAY…. I TELL THEM THAT THIS LAND IS OURS AND THE **WASICHUS** HAVE NO RIGHT TO IT. WE MUST FIGHT FOR WHAT **WAKAN TANKA** HAS GIVEN US.

THE SOLDIERS ARE CLOSING IN ON US WITH SCOUTS FROM OUR OWN PEOPLE! WE ARE ALMOST OUT OF AMMUNITION… MAYBE WE CAN LIVE IN PEACE SOMEWHERE ELSE MAYBE IN **GRANDMOTHER'S LAND** THERE ARE **WASICHUS** WITH STRAIGHT TONGUES, WHO DON'T KILL INDIANS. LET'S JOIN SITTING BULL AND OUR RELATIVES THERE!

YOU BELIEVE IN PEACE, COUSIN, AND I HOPE YOU'LL FIND IT. BUT THE FIGHT AGAINST THE INVADER CONTINUES, EVEN IF THE SHADOW OF DEATH HANGS OVER US. I MUST STAY HERE, IN THE COUNTRY OF OUR FATHERS.

IN THE SPRINGTIME, CRAZY HORSE AND HIS STARVING BAND SURRENDERED TO THE PROMISE OF A RESERVATION OF THEIR OWN CHOOSING. LIKE SO MANY OTHER *WASICHU* PROMISES, IT WAS NEVER HONORED. MEANWHILE, I LED OUR SMALL BAND TO THE NORTH, FLEEING FROM THE SOLDIERS ACROSS THE COUNTRY OF OUR FOES, THE *CROWS* AND *BLACKFEET,* TO JOIN SITTING BULL....

HEYAH!

IN *GRANDMOTHER'S LAND,* FAR FROM THE SOLDIERS, WE LIVED IN THE OLD WAY, HUNTING BISON....

I KEPT ON HEALING OUR PEOPLE....

WAKAN TANKA! HEAR MY VOICE!

MY HUSBAND DOESN'T WANT TO EAT WITH HIS WOMAN AND CHILDREN?

THE WINDS AND THE BIRDS BRING A MESSAGE FROM OUR COUNTRY...

...A DARK MESSAGE! THEY TALK ABOUT MY COUSIN CRAZY HORSE! MY HEART FEELS HEAVY! I FEEL WINDS OF PAIN AND SADNESS BLOWING UPON OUR PEOPLE....

A LONG TIME AFTERWARD, I LEARNED THAT OUR GREATEST LEADER, MY COUSIN CRAZY HORSE, HAD BEEN MURDERED BY THE SOLDIERS AT FORT ROBINSON.[1]

[1] ON SEPTEMBER 5, 1877

WAKAN TANKA! HELP US TO FIND MEAT!

THAT WAS A VERY COLD WINTER, WITH MANY BLIZZARDS. GAME WAS HARD TO FIND. MANY OF OUR HORSES FROZE TO DEATH, AND WE ALMOST STARVED....

WAKAN TANKA, ONSHIMALA YE OYATE WANI WACHIN CHA![1]

HUNGER AND SICKNESS ARE DESTROYING MY PEOPLE! I HAVE LOST MY FATHER, MY BROTHER, A CHILD! WE ARE IN DESPAIR... WAKAN TANKA! HELP US TO MAKE THE TREE OF LIFE BLOSSOM AND REMAKE THE SACRED CIRCLE!

HOPE CAME FROM THE SOUTH WHEN WOVOKA, THE PAIUTE HOLY MAN, PREACHED THE NEW RELIGION....

ALL THE INDIANS MUST DANCE, DANCE TO BE IN TOUCH WITH THE SACRED WORLD. A NEW WORLD IS COMING, IN WHICH ALL OUR DEAD WILL COME BACK TO LIFE, THE WHITE MAN WILL DISAPPEAR, AND THE BUFFALO WILL RETURN! THE GREAT SPIRIT WILL COME! WE WILL LIVE IN PEACE AND PLENTY!

GREAT SPIRIT, BE MERCIFUL TO ME, THAT MY PEOPLE MAY LIVE.

ONE AFTER ANOTHER, THE PLAINS TRIBES JOINED THE NEW RELIGION. THE LAKOTAS, TOO, STARTED DANCING.

HE IS THE ONE WHO MAKES THE SACRED THINGS...HE IS THE ONE WHO MAKES THE SACRED SHIRT... HE IS THE ONE WHO MADE THE PIPE...SAYS THE FATHER, SAYS THE FATHER!

AT ALL THE AGENCIES, THE INDIANS ARE BECOMING FANATICAL ABOUT THE GHOST DANCE....THEY'RE GOING CRAZY! THEY BELIEVE THAT THE SIGNS PAINTED ON THEIR SHIRTS WILL MAKE THEM BULLETPROOF!

THE WASICHUS BECAME FRIGHTENED...

WE MUST AVOID AN UPRISING... WE'LL ARREST THE LEADERS OF THE MOVEMENT AND BREAK IT!

DURING THE WINTER, THE SOLDIERS INVADED THE RESERVATIONS....

YOU MUST STOP DANCING! BREAK CAMP AND RETURN TO THE AGENCY! THIS IS ORDERED BY THE GREAT WHITE FATHER IN WASHINGTON!

THE MOST POTENTIALLY DANGEROUS OF THEM IS SITTING BULL...WE MUST NEUTRALIZE HIM AT ANY COST!

48

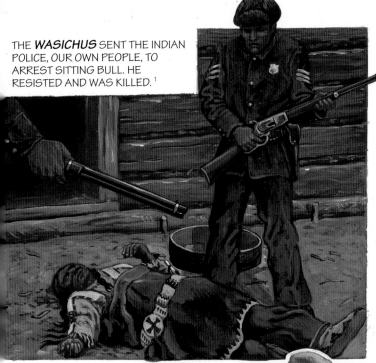

THE *WASICHUS* SENT THE INDIAN POLICE, OUR OWN PEOPLE, TO ARREST SITTING BULL. HE RESISTED AND WAS KILLED. [1]

AFTER THAT, THINGS GOT WORSE....

VERY MANY SOLDIERS LEFT FOR BIG FOOT'S CAMP, WITH **WAGON GUNS**. [2] OUR PEOPLE SAY THE TROOPS WILL KILL ALL THE INDIANS THIS TIME, SO THEY'RE PREPARING THEMSELVES FOR WAR, MY FATHER.

BIG FOOT IS VERY ILL AND HIS BAND IS STARVING. SOMETHING TERRIBLE IS GOING TO HAPPEN! GET READY, MY SON! MAYBE WE, TOO, WILL HAVE TO FIGHT FOR OUR LIVES!

[1] NOVEMBER 19, 1890

[2] CANNONS

HEY-HEY-HEY! THE SOLDIERS ARE KILLING OUR PEOPLE!!! THEY'VE ATTACKED BIG FOOT'S CAMP!

BAM! BAM! BOUM!

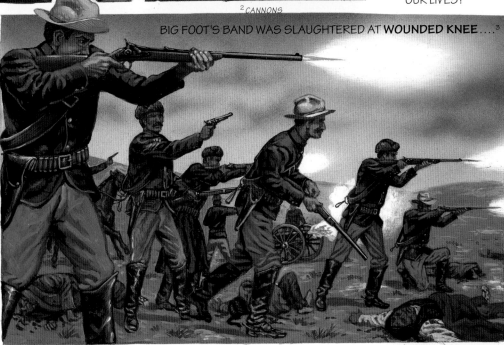

BIG FOOT'S BAND WAS SLAUGHTERED AT **WOUNDED KNEE**....[3]

TAKE COURAGE! THEY'RE OUR PEOPLE!

GREAT SPIRIT!! **OH GREAT SPIRIT!!!**

[3] ON DECEMBER 29, 1890, ABOUT 200 *LAKOTAS*, MAINLY WOMEN AND CHILDREN, WERE SLAUGHTERED BY THE 7TH CAVALRY.

AND AT THAT MOMENT, THE **POWERS** LEFT ME....

WHILE MY BLOOD REDDENED THE SNOW, I REALIZED THAT OUR PEOPLE'S HOPE HAD VANISHED FOREVER. MANY SOLDIERS CAME AND THE WARRIORS HAD TO RETREAT, TAKING ME WITH THEM. I WAS SERIOUSLY WOUNDED, BUT UNDER THE CARE OF OLD HOLLOW HORN, THE HEALER, I RECOVERED.

51

THE WINTER WAS EXTREMELY HARSH. CORNERED BY THE WELL-EQUIPPED AND WELL-FED TROOPS OF **BEAR COAT,** WE WERE SHORT OF AMMUNITION AND STARVING...

THE WAR DID NOT LAST LONG...AND SO THE LAST OF THE **LAKOTAS** SURRENDERED [2]. OLD CHIEF RED CLOUD SPOKE...

MY BROTHERS, THIS IS A VERY HARD WINTER. OUR WOMEN AND CHILDREN ARE FREEZING AND STARVING. IF THIS WAS SUMMER, WE COULD STAND AND FIGHT TO THE END. BUT IT WILL BE TOO HARD FOR OUR WEAK ONES. TO SAVE OUR PEOPLE FROM EXTERMINATION, WE MUST MAKE PEACE.

[1] GENERAL NELSON MILES   [2] JANUARY 16, 1891

IN LESS THAN A MOON, EVERYTHING CAME TO AN END. WE WENT TO PINE RIDGE AND SURRENDERED. OUR DREAM OF FREEDOM WAS OVER.

MANY, MANY SEASONS HAVE PASSED. I'VE SEEN MY CHILDREN, MY GRANDCHILDREN, AND MY GREAT GRANDCHILDREN GROW UP IN THE RESERVATION. I'VE SEEN THE SACRED HOOP OF THE NATION BROKEN UNDER THE PRESSURE OF THE **WASICHUS'** WORLD. I'VE SEEN OUR WORLD CHANGE WITH ALL THEIR MACHINES. I'VE SEEN OUR PEOPLE ADOPT THE **WASICHUS'** WAYS AND LOSE THE SPIRITUAL POWER THAT LINKS US FROM OUR MOTHER EARTH TO THE GREAT SPIRIT. I'VE SEEN MANY, MANY SAD CHANGES IN THE **LAKOTA** WORLD....

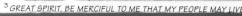

[1] CARS

[2] IT IS SO INDEED.

[3] GREAT SPIRIT, BE MERCIFUL TO ME THAT MY PEOPLE MAY LIVE.

SERGIO MACEDO

Afterword

IT IS THE ARTIST or poet who generally reaches the people in an artistic way. And the images of poets and artists help to say things in the most lasting way.

In Sergio Macedo's book called *Lakota,* the art of words, the art of painting, and the art within a culture all come together in making a statement. At first the graphic artwork just grabs the eye. Then you begin to look into it more and more carefully, and you see that the integrity of the Lakota people is there, and that Sergio is using a medium that bypasses the educational system to teach something worthwhile.

I first met Sergio at the Kayapo village of Metuktire on the Xingu River in Brazil when I was on a world tour with the rock singer Sting, and we became acquainted and have kept in contact for years. I always thought he was a great artist. I can praise him as an artist, and I can praise him for having done a considerable amount of research into the Lakota culture. He is excellent, so completely thorough in his search into the history and culture. I see a lot of Black Elk in this book, which has a strong historical connection even though some parts are fiction. Sergio's artwork is outstanding, and because of it I think his message will reach some people who might not be reached otherwise.

— Floyd Red Crow Westerman

About the Artist

SERGIO MACEDO was born in Além Paraiba, Brazil in 1951. At the age of four, he produced his first book by drawing a copy of the Classic Comic version of *The Last of the Mohicans*.

"Then when I was twelve or thirteen," he says, "the idea of drawing the history of each tribe in South and North America began to grow in my mind." And now *Lakota* is the first in that series of illustrated histories.

Macedo has visited many Native American communities, from the rainforests of the Amazon to the deserts of the southwestern United States. Respect and meticulous accuracy are his goals, and every detail in his work is based on fact. "I feel a strong connection with the Indian way of life," he says. "In *Lakota* I tried to show that the Lakota, like other native cultures, have a very rich spiritual side, which White people often neglect."

Macedo prefers to communicate through pictures: "This is my language. It comes like a film in my mind. I can see everything moving, like a real film. I can hear talking. But the text comes last. First comes the motion, then the sketches."

An artist who has established an international reputation, Macedo paints in acrylic on paper. He has published more than a dozen graphic novels in Europe and the Americas, and his individual paintings have also been exhibited. Besides Brazil, he has also lived in France, and since 1982 he has made his home on the island of Moorea in French Polynesia, where he lives with his wife, Nita Faraire.

"I'm trying, with my limitations, to show Native American history," he says, "and to show their bond with the spiritual world and the powers of nature. I'd like my books to be read by young people—including young Lakotas, young Apaches. That's what I have in my heart."

References

Andrist, Ralph K. *The Long Death: The Last Days of the Plains Indians*. New York: Macmillan, 1964.

Brown, Joseph (ed.) As told by Black Elk. *The Sacred Pipe: Black Elk's Account of the Seven Rites of the Oglala Sioux*. Norman, OK: University of Oklahoma Press, 1989.

Brown, Vinson. *Crazy Horse: Hoka Hey: It's a Good Time to Die!* Happy Camp, CA: Naturegraph Publishers, Inc., 1978.

Deer, John L. and Richard Erdoes. *Lame Deer, Seeker of Visions: The Life of a Sioux Medicine Man*. New York: Pocket Books, 1984.

Dillon, Richard. *North American Indian Wars*. Edison, NJ: Book Sales, Inc., 1993.

Dubois, Daniel and Yves Berger. *Les Indiens des Plaines*. Editions Dargaud, 1984.

Ewers, John C. *Artists of the Old West*. New York: Doubleday, 1965.

Fire Lame Deer, Archie. *Inipi*. L'Or du Temps Editions, 1987.

Hassrick, Royal. *The Sioux: Life and Customs of a Warrior Society*. Norman, OK: University of Oklahoma Press, 1964.

Hill, Ruth Beebe. *Hanta Yo*. New York: Warner Books, 1964.

Hyde, George. *A Sioux Chronicle*. Norman, OK: University of Oklahoma Press, 1956.

Neihardt, John G. *Black Elk Speaks: Being the Life Story of a Holy Man of the Oglala Sioux*. Lincoln, NE: University of Nebraska Press, 1932. Revised edition, 1979.

Sandoz, Mari. *Crazy Horse: The Strange Man of the Oglalas*. Lincoln, NE: University of Nebraska Press, 1961.

Standing Bear, Luther. (E. A. Brininstool and Richard N. Ellis, eds.) *My People the Sioux*. Lincoln, NE: University of Nebraska Press, 1975.

Taylor, Collin and William Sturtevant. *The Native Americans: The Indigenous People of North America*. (n.p.) Salamander Books, 1991.

Wellman, Paul I. *The Indian Wars of the West*. Garden City, NY: Doubleday, 1954.